Cards had been posted,
twinkly lights had been put
up and Christmas trees
had been decorated.

5

There was also another special event taking place on this busy day - the Christmas baking competition! Tasty goodies of all kinds would be judged, with the VERY BEST declared the overall winner!

6

To **Noah**
The star of the story!

From

Noah was VERY excited as it was the day before Christmas Eve, and everyone was rushing around getting everything ready for the celebrations ahead.

This year's very important judge was Santa Claus, who had been flown in by Rudolph on his sleigh.

7

All the bakers
were busy making
their goodies.

There were mince pies,
yule logs, festive cakes,
scrumptious puddings
and of course
Christmas cookies.

8

Noah, who was on Santa's nice list and had been specially invited to watch the baking competition, noticed that one of the contestants, a little gingerbread boy, was crying. "Hello, what's the matter?" Noah asked kindly.

The gingerbread boy sobbed to Noah that he was ready to decorate his gingerbread cookies but that all his icing, raisins and chocolate buttons had gone MISSING! "Don't worry," Noah gently told the gingerbread boy. "I will help you to look for them."

The gingerbread boy jumped for joy, then pointed to the clock on the wall. They didn't have much time as Santa would soon start the judging.

Noah began to look for clues - perhaps one of the other bakers had hidden the decorations!

They looked in Big Bear's back pocket.

They looked under Happy Hare's hat.

They even looked behind Eager Elf's ears, but the decorations were nowhere to be found!

Then, just as they were about to give up, clever Noah noticed a little trail of icing sugar on the floor leading to the back door and it had some very strange-looking footprints in it!

13

They followed the footprints
and as they stepped outside they saw
some icing splats and blobs, and a few
raisins that had been dropped.

14

"Can you hear that?" Noah asked the gingerbread boy.

There was a loud crunching followed by an even louder munching sound coming from Santa's sleigh.

15

Chewing on a crunchy carrot while
singing some rather out of tune
Christmas songs was Rudolph -
and he was busily decorating
reindeer shaped cookies with the
missing decorations!

"Rudolph, what are you doing?" exclaimed Noah. "The gingerbread boy needs those decorations!"

Rudolph explained that he just wanted to borrow them so he could enter the competition himself.

18

"I have a brilliant idea!" said Noah. "You can help us decorate the cookies."

They all rushed back into the hall to get started as time was running out.

19

Icing, chocolate buttons and raisins flew everywhere as one by one the tasty gingerbread cookies were decorated and finished in the nick of time.

The three looked on nervously as Santa came to the table to inspect all the entries.

20

Then to their complete surprise
he announced that Noah,
Rudolph and the gingerbread
boy were the winners... and to
Rudolph's dismay the first prize
was a trip in Santa's sleigh!

The end

21

COLOR
ME IN